Lily lived in a big, old, dusty house.

She lived there with her Great Aunt Maud, who knitted things.

The house had spiders under sofas and beetles between bed legs.

But Lily liked it.

It was Lily's birthday morning.

Happy Birthday Lily.
follow the arrows to
find your presents

She jumped out of bed,

got dressed

and
ran
downstairs.

There she
found a
note.

Beside it was a small arrow.
Lily followed the arrow upstairs.
The trail took her all around the house.
Which rooms did she look in?

THE INCREDIBLE PRESENT

Harriet Castor

Designed by Maria Wheatley

Illustrated by Norman Young

Language and Reading Consultant: David Wray
(Education Department, University of Exeter, England)

Series Editor: Gaby Waters

First published in 1994 by Usborne Publishing Ltd, Usborne House, 83-85 Saffron Hill, London EC1N 8RT, England.
Printed in Portugal. UE. First published in America March 1995.

Lily ended up in the sitting room.
Great Aunt Maud was there.

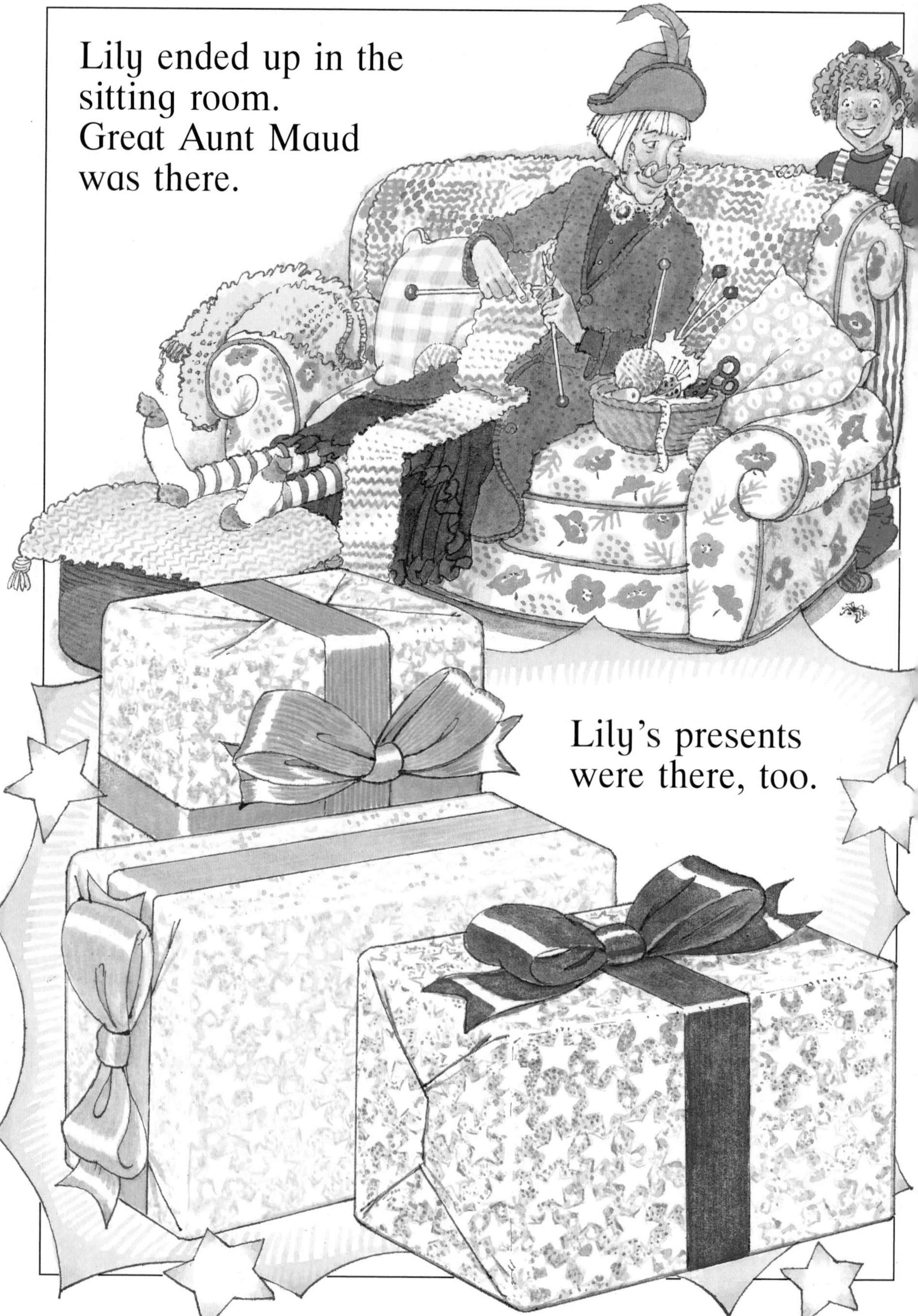

Lily's presents were there, too.

She SQUISHED them and SQUEEZED them.

Then she lined them up,

and

piled

them

high.

Next, she got out her X-RAY glasses.

What could she see?

At last, Lily opened her presents.

The first present wasn't a super long range telescope.

The second present wasn't a giraffe.

The third present wasn't a toy garage.

Then Lily saw one last present.

Where had it come from?

The parcel was from
Lily’s Ma and Pa.

Ma and Pa were explorers.
Lily didn't mind when
they went away.
They always came
back with exciting.
stories to tell.

They had
set off on an
expedition to
the jungle.

Will be back
in time for
your birthday.
Love Ma
and Pa xxx

They were due
back soon.
Lily hoped it said
on the parcel when
they'd be home.
Did it?

Lily wondered what Ma and Pa had sent her from their travels.

A dinosaur tooth?
A rainbow hamster?

An ice cream plant?

She opened the parcel. Inside was a small bag.

There was a label on it.

Lily tried it out.

There was something strange about the crayons.

What was it?

Lily wrote a list of everything she wanted to ask the bag for.

Pet snail
Bubble bath with the biggest bubbles in the world
55 Bowls of pink icing
P.S. you can only ask for six things.

Then she noticed a second label.

There were five choices left. Lily thought hard.

She hated making her bed every morning, so she asked for

A bed making robot.

But it didn't do quite what she wanted.

What did it do?

Lily tried again.
She asked for
A space buggy.
Oh no!

Lily's fourth choice was

A witch's kit with real spells in it.
pong
poo
wiff
Witch's cat with real smells in it

But the bag must have heard her wrong.

What did she get instead?

Lily hated having cabbage for dinner, so next she asked for

A zapper that turns all your greens into chocolate ice-cream.

Lily tried it out.

It worked!

But everything green had been zapped, including

Great Aunt Maud's hat

and most of her garden.

Lily, do something!
Happy Birthday Lily, love Ma and Pa xxx

Then Lily had an idea.

Can you guess what it was?

For her last choice,
Lily asked for

Ma and Pa
to come home.

They arrived in a flash,
and Lily told them what had happened.

We'd better put
the bag into
reverse.

Pa turned the bag inside out.

Then Ma said something complicated.

Red
Green
Light Blue
Pa and Ma except for you asked Lily that everything back take please, bag dear.

Can you figure out what it meant?
(Clue: try reading the sentence back to front.)

The grass was grass again.
The robot and his beds had gone.
Lily couldn't smell the cat anymore.
Sniff
Sniff
And she couldn't hear any alien babies squawking.

Sorry about that. It was our first invention.
We've decided to give up exploring and do something else instead.
William and Kitty Puddleton
EXPLORERS
Inventors
N
E
S

Lily hoped this meant they weren't going away again.

Then she spotted something that told her the answer.

What was it?

Soon all was quiet.

You'd never have guessed what a strange birthday it had been.

Except that Great Aunt Maud was never quite so fond of her green hat again.

It always made her ears a little sticky.